Two Tracks in the Snow

by Louella Bryant

Illustrated by Todd Fargo

Jason and Nordic Publishers
Hollidaysburg, Pennsylvania

More Turtle Books
For children with disabilities and their friends

Andy Finds a Turtle
Danny and the Merry-go-round
How about a Hug
Patrick and Emma Lou
Cookie
A Smile from Andy
Andy Opens Wide
Sarah's Surprise
Buddy's Shadow
Fair and Square
When I Grow Up
The Night Search

Text and Illustrations copyright © 2004 Jason & Nordic Publishers

Library of Congress Catalog Number   2003115493

Two tracks in the snow / Louella Bryant : illustrated by Todd Fargo.
Fiction. subjects include: Spina Bifida/ friendship/ skiing/
winter snow sports/ disabilities

Paper: ISBN 0-944727-45-X
Library binding: ISBN 0-944727-46-8

Printed in the U.S.A.
on acid free paper

Dedicated to
Kathy Chandler
and
AbilityPlus

as well as all the other
enthusiastic instructors everywhere
who make winter sports possible
for children with disabilities.

The mountain looked like a chocolate cupcake with vanilla ski trails dripping down the sides.

Inside the lodge, Will worked his feet into his new blue ski boots, but he couldn't close the buckles.

"Lift your foot up here," someone said. "I'll do that for you."

Will looked up and saw a boy in a wheelchair.

"I guess I could use some help," Will said, and he raised his boot.

"My name's Ari," the boy said. He pulled Will's foot onto his lap.

Ari snapped the buckles closed.

"Thanks. I'm Will."

"Is this your first time, Will?" Ari asked.

"Yes, but I'm sure I can do it." Will tromped in a circle, trying out his boots.

"I fell a lot my first time," Ari said.

"You ski?" Will asked. "How?"

"Sure," Ari said. "Special equipment. I don't let spina bifida stop me."

"Spina what?" Will asked.

"Something happened in my spine before I was born. My legs don't work right. But the rest of me works great," Ari said.

"Oh, but how do you ski?" Will asked.

"Special equipment—a monoski," Ari said. Then he waved. "See you on the slopes."

What's a monoski, Will wondered?

Outside, Will clicked his heels into the bindings of his new red skis. He saw a man helping Ari into a seat attached to a single ski. How could Ari get down the mountain on a one-ski chair?

Ari held two poles with short skis on the bottoms—too small to be much help, Will thought.

"Good luck, Will," Ari yelled. A tiger tail dangled from his helmet.

The man pushed Ari to the big chair lift. It caught under the monoski, and up Ari went, seat and all.

Soon Will saw the tiger tail bouncing as Ari glided down the hill. His monoski made S-shapes never even wobbling. When he reached the bottom, Ari skied back to the chairlift and went up again.

Will wanted to ride the big chairlift. He could hardly wait until he was slicing S-shapes in the snow.

"Ready for ski school?" a woman said. "I'm Tracy, your instructor."

When Will shuffled toward his ski lesson, he lost his balance and toppled over. Wiggling around, he pushed himself up. He slid two feet, and down he went again.

"Everybody needs help sometimes," Tracy said. She hoisted him up and guided him to where the others waited.

"First, we make a wedge," she said. "Like a pizza—toes together, weight forward."

The other skiers followed her, but Will trailed at the end of the line. This skiing business was harder than he thought. He keeled over, the red skis sticking in the air.

"Come on, Will," Tracy said.

"I can't," Will said.

Ari skied over on his monoski. "There's no such thing as can't," he said.

"I'll never be a skier," Will grumbled.

"If I can do it, anyone can," Ari said.

Tracy clapped her gloves together. "Say, Ari, why don't you see what you can do for Will?"

"Okay," Ari said.

Will wondered how sitting down skiing could be the same as standing up skiing, but he gritted his teeth. He had come to ski, and ski he would.

"Why don't we take the beginner lift?" Ari said. The double seats wobbled up a gentle slope.

"Any baby could ride the beginner lift," Will said.

"Then let's go," Ari called.

The lift person helped Ari onto a chair. Tracy and Will rode the chair behind him. Will watched the snow speed under his skis. The sun made the powdery snow sparkle.

From the top, the slope looked steeper. "Gravity does all the work," Ari told Will. "Watch me."

He started down the hill, turning in wide arcs. Ari made skiing look easy.

"You try it now," he yelled up to Will.

Will didn't want Ari to think he was scared, so he pushed off with his poles. He shifted toward the right and skied left across the slope. When he got to the pine trees, he shifted his weight again and turned to the right.

Suddenly Will was skiing.

His red skis whooshed against the snow. The wind stung his face. The trees whizzed by in a green blur. He tried to pull his ski tips together to slow down, but one crossed the other. His legs crossed, his arms crossed, his eyes crossed, and he twirled, rolling and tumbling down the hill.

SNAP!

A red ski soared over his head. His glove fell off, and—PLOP! He landed face-first in a snow bank.

Will rolled over and sat up. His mouth was filled with snow. His gloves were filled with snow. Snow packed his collar and the silver buckles of his blue boots—but where were the red skis?

"Lose something?" A red ski balanced across Ari's legs.

"Oh, I give up," Will pouted. "I'll just sit in the lodge and watch everyone else have fun."

"I have another idea," said Ari. He waved a ski pole at Tracy, who was just finishing a lesson.

"I think Will needs some special equipment," Ari said.

Tracy winked at Ari and led Will to the rental shop. She traded in the red skis and the blue boots for a green snowboard and snowboard boots. Then she helped Will strap his boots to the board.

Will fell lots of times, but the snow was soft and he managed to get up. Snowboarding was a lot like riding his skateboard at home.

Finally, Ari said, "I think you're ready for the big chairlift."

Yes, Will thought. The big chairlift.

Will got into position next to Ari on his monoski, and when the chair came around, the lift helper put them on. In seconds, they were so high that the skiers below looked like small toys. Will spread his arms—he felt like he was flying.

When they reached the mountain-top, Will was ready. "Remember to lean and turn," Ari said.

Then they took off down the slope, turning and gliding. Will fell a few more times, but Ari always waited for him.

When they got to the bottom, Will said, "Let's go again!"

Will and Ari skied and skied and once, Will went from top to bottom without falling.

At the end of the day, Ari's father met him with the wheelchair.

"See you next weekend?" Ari asked.

"You bet," said Will.

Before he went into the lodge to meet his mother, Will looked back at the mountain.

Two tracks made graceful S-curves
side by side in the new snow.

JUV SPECIAL NEEDS PHYSICAL
Bryant, Louella, 1947-
Two tracks in the snow

Concordia College Library
Bronxville, NY 10708